For Martin,
Lil, Mimi, and
Debbie Pope

Four Winds Press • New York

Kitten for
a Day

by Ezra Jack Keats

Are you a kitten?

Uh huh--I think so.

O.K. Follow us!

Lap, lap, lap

Splash !

Lick, lick, lick

Slurp!

Meeeeoooow!

Meee...rrruff!

Ooops!

Eeek!

Eeeeek!

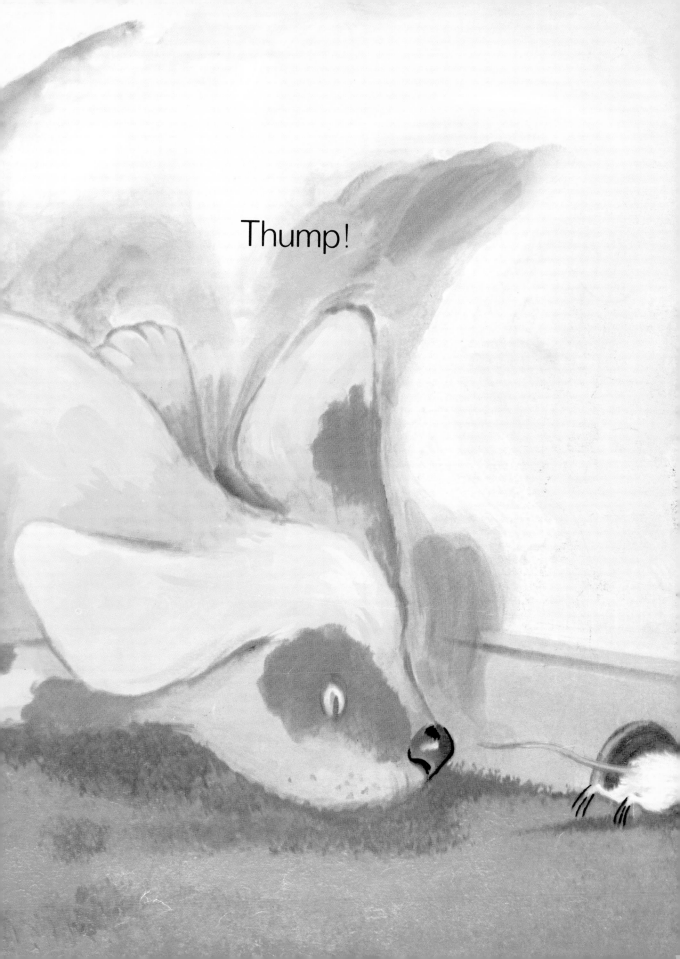

Thump!

Sorry !

Puppy,
come home
right now!

Next time,
let's all
be puppies !

Library of Congress Cataloging in Publication Data

Keats, Ezra Jack.
  Kitten for a day.

  Summary: A puppy joins a litter of kittens in
their fun and games for one day.
  [1. Cats—Fiction. 2. Dogs—Fiction] I. Title.
PZ7.K2253Ki 1982 [E] 81-69518
ISBN 0-590-07813-5   AACR2

Published by Four Winds Press.
A division of Scholastic Inc., New York, N.Y.
Library of Congress Catalog Card Number: 81-69518
1   2   3   4   5   86   85   84   83   82